Farmer Falgu Goes on a Trip

Chitra Soundar
Kanika Nair

Cluck cluck!
Moo moo! Woof woof!
Quack quack!

Farmer Falgu's farm was **noisy**.

"What a racket," said Farmer Falgu.
"I'm going to look for silence."

Farmer Falgu cleaned his cart.
He washed his oxen.
He packed some lunch.

Farmer Falgu set off on a trip to find silence.

On his way, Farmer Falgu
met an old man.

"Please can I ride with you?"
asked the old man.
"My sack is very heavy."

"Climb on,"

said Farmer Falgu.

Then they set off.

The old man took out his drum
and started to play.

Dum-dum
went the drum.

Trot-trot
went the oxen.

The old man sang a funny song. Farmer Falgu
forgot about silence and joined along.

Just after noon, they passed a
snake charmer on the way.
"Can I get a ride too?" he asked.

"Hop on,"

said Farmer Falgu.

"Move, move,"

said the snake charmer.

The old man moved inside.

Farmer Falgu, the old man, and the
snake charmer set off again.

Phee-phee played the snake charmer on his pipe.

Dum-dum went the drums.

Trot-trot went the oxen.

The old man sang another song.
Farmer Falgu forgot about silence and sang along.

The sun had begun to set.
A dance troupe waved from the roadside.
"Will you take us to the next town?"
asked the dancers.

"Jump in,"

said Farmer Falgu.

"Move, move, move,"

said the dancers.

The snake charmer shuffled inside.
The old man moved inside.
Farmer Falgu, the old man, the snake charmer
and the dance troupe set off again.

Tap-tap-tap
the dancers tapped their feet.

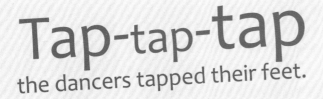

Phee-phee
played the snake charmer on his pipe.

Dum-dum
went the drums.

Trot-trot
went the oxen.

The old man began a new song.
Farmer Falgu forgot about silence
and chorused along.

The moon was out when they reached the next town.
The dancers jumped off near the fair.
The snake charmer got down at the town-square.
The old man too, parted ways near the riverside.

Farmer Falgu set off again to look for silence.

The night was quiet.

"This is silence!" thought Farmer Falgu.
"Just the thing I'm looking for."

He stopped the cart and closed his eyes.
He listened to the quiet night.

As he listened some more,
he heard crickets chirping,
frogs croaking,
the wind whispering.
He heard rustling leaves,
grunting lizards
and sleepy bird calls.

Farmer Falgu groaned.
Was he ever going to find

silence?

He thought about his farm,
where wind rustled by the hay-bales,
the chickens dropped their eggs
and the pigs sloshed in their pens.

"Ah!" said Farmer Falgu with a smile.

"My farm is **not noisy.** It is **happy!**"

He turned his cart around and set off home.

Trot-trot went the oxen.

La-la sang Farmer Falgu.

Farmer Falgu Goes on a Trip

Text: Chitra Soundar
Illustrations: Kanika Nair

Karadi Tales Company Pvt. Ltd.
3A Dev Regency, 11 First Main Road,
Gandhinagar, Adyar, Chennai 600 020
Ph: +91 44 4205 4243
email: contact@karaditales.com
Website: www.karaditales.com

Printed in India

Cataloging - in - Publication information:

Chitra Soundar
Farmer Falgu Goes on a Trip / Chitra Soundar;
Illustrated by Kanika Nair
p.32; color illustrations; 23 x 20.5 cm.

1. Travel--Juvenile literature. 2. Conduct of life--Humor.
3. Conduct of life--Juvenile fiction.

PZ7   [E]

JUV001000   JUVENILE FICTION / Action & Adventure / General
JUV002090   JUVENILE FICTION / Animals / Farm Animals
JUV030020   JUVENILE FICTION / People & Places / Asia
JUV025000   JUVENILE FICTION / Lifestyles / Farm & Ranch Life

ISBN 978-81-8190-347-1

Printed in India
Distributed in the United States by
Consortium Book Sales & Distribution
www.cbsd.com

CHITRA SOUNDAR

Chitra hails from India, resides in London and lives in imaginary worlds weaved out of stories. She has written over twenty books for children aged 3 to 10 years old. Chitra also loves to retell folktales, legends and ancient tales from the Indian sub-continent. While she dabbles in chapter books, her first love is picture books.

KANIKA NAIR

Kanika Nair has always had a passion for illustration. After receiving a bachelor's degree in Communication Design from Pearl Academy of Fashion, New Delhi, she began working as a freelance illustrator, writer and designer of children's books. She loves to incorporate various insights about children that she has collected over years into her illustrations. The Indian cultural canvas has always fascinated her and this is quite evident in her style of illustration.